THE STRANGE CASE OF
DR JEKYLL AND
MR HYDE

A DORLING KINDERSLEY BOOK

AN ADAPTATION FOR CHILDREN OF THE ORIGINAL BOOK

Project Editor David Pickering
Art Editor Mary Walsh
Senior Editor Marie Greenwood
Senior Designer Jane Thomas
Production Katy Holmes
Managing Art Editor Chris Fraser
Picture Research Louise Thomas
DTP Designer Kim Browne
Consultant Simon Adams

First published in Great Britain in 1997 by
Dorling Kindersley Limited, 9 Henrietta Street, London WC2E 8PS

Visit us on the World Wide Web at http://www.dk.com

A CIP catalogue record for this book is available from the British Library.

ISBN 0-7513-7085-1

Colour reproduction by Bright Arts in Hong Kong
Printed by Graphicom in Italy

EYEWITNESS ◉ CLASSICS

THE STRANGE CASE OF
DR JEKYLL AND MR HYDE

ROBERT LOUIS STEVENSON

Adapted by MICHAEL LAWRENCE

Illustrated
by IAN ANDREW

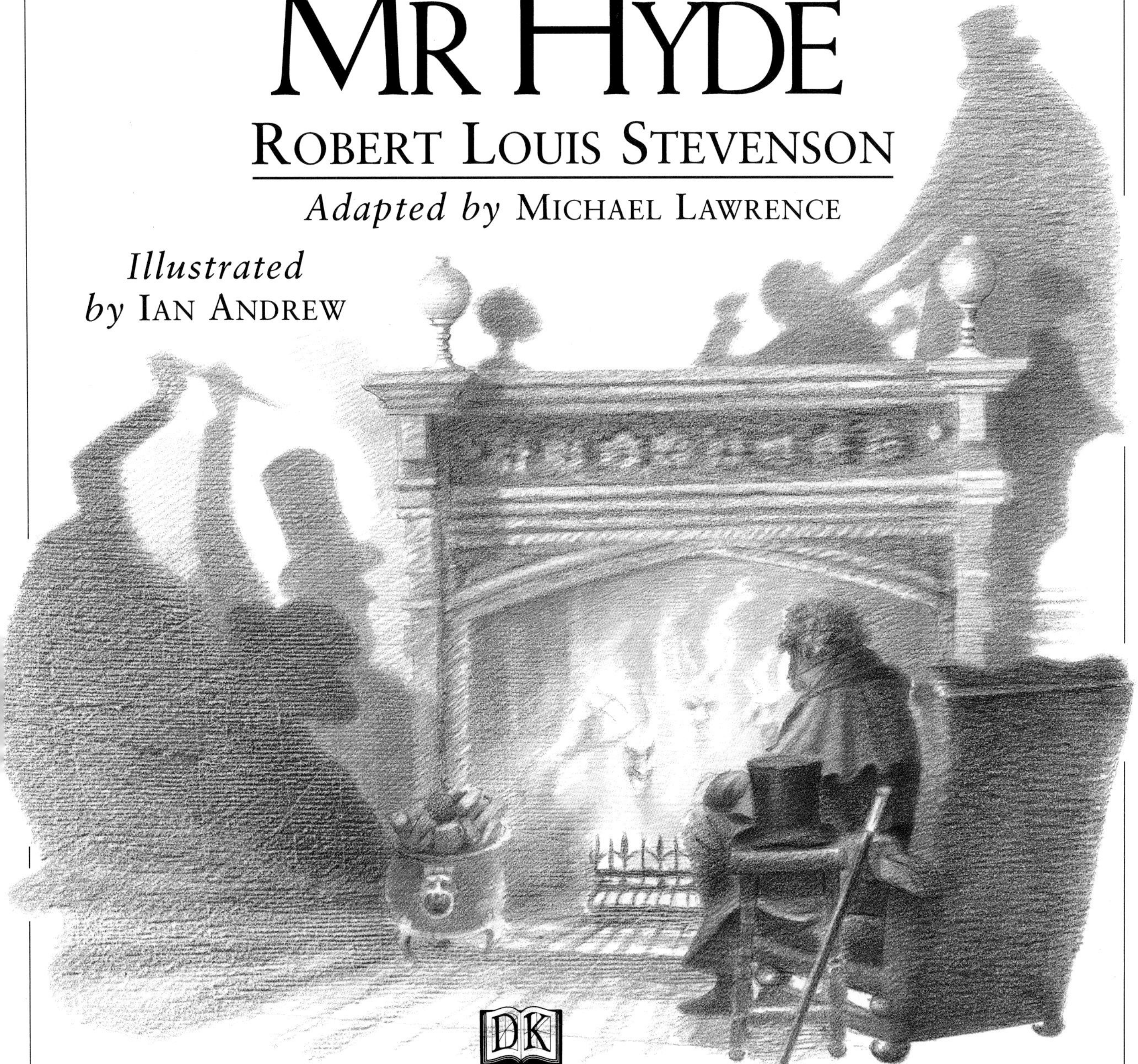

DK

DORLING KINDERSLEY

LONDON • NEW YORK • STUTTGART • MOSCOW

CONTENTS

Dr Henry Jekyll

Mr Gabriel Utterson

Mr Edward Hyde

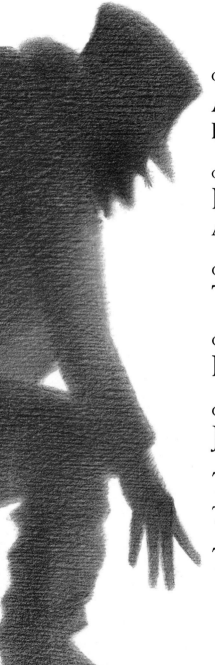

Dr Hastie Lanyon

*Poole,
Dr Jekyll's butler*

INTRODUCTION

EVERYONE HAS HEARD of Jekyll and Hyde. They have moved beyond literary fame into the realm of legend. But what our culture has made of them is not quite what their author originally intended. This edition explores both the original book that Robert Louis Stevenson wrote and the myths that followed.

Few children will read that original because, although short, it is deliberately complicated. Stevenson wanted to keep his adult readers guessing. This Eyewitness Classic edition simplifies the book's complex structure, introducing a narrator while keeping as many of Stevenson's own words as possible. At the same time, it sets the story firmly in its context, showing where Stevenson found the inspiration for this extraordinary tale.

Information pages explain how Stevenson's childhood in Edinburgh and his rebellion against his strict upbringing eventually led his imagination to the foggy, lamplit streets haunted by Edward Hyde. Fact and picture columns explain the background to the people and places mentioned in the story, the grand houses of the rich and the other, darker side of London. Photographs, paintings, and film stills illustrate the impact of *Dr Jekyll and Mr Hyde* in the century since its publication.

Dr Jekyll's friend Mr Utterson will introduce you to the worthy doctor, his famous friend and fellow doctor, Hastie Lanyon, and his faithful butler Poole. Above all, you will meet that unique and unforgettable character, Mr Edward Hyde.

A painting of a London street at night, by John Atkinson Grimshaw (1836–1893)

THE TWO FACES OF LONDON

In 1886, when *Dr Jekyll and Mr Hyde* was first published, London was the wealthiest city in the world. Dr Jekyll and his friends were well-off, respected men, working in respectable professions and living in the rich West End, one of the smartest areas of the city. They had little contact with the crime and the harshness of life in the poorer areas of London, until their lives were disturbed by Mr Edward Hyde.

The Victorian gentleman

The main characters in the story are all "gentlemen", men of high social status, expected to live honourable lives. They live in smart houses looked after by servants. Two of the gentlemen, Jekyll and Lanyon, are successful doctors; one, Utterson, is a lawyer.

A gentleman doctor

The vast metropolis

London was the biggest city in the world, with a population of about four million. At night, it was an eerier, emptier city than it is today. It was less well-lit, with less nightlife and fewer people on the dark evening streets.

A view of Fleet Street in central London

The grand facades of Cavendish Square houses announced their owners' wealth.

Jekyll's house was very grand but the square he lived in was not as smart as Cavendish Square.

REGENT STREET

OXFORD CIRCUS

A black top hat completed a gentleman's evening dress.

Cavendish Square

Dr Lanyon lived in Cavendish Square, a centre of medicine where many doctors and surgeons lived. Dr Jekyll lived in an unnamed square not far away, and Mr Utterson also lived in the neighbourhood. The area around Cavendish Square was a very smart part of the West End.

Formal evening dress included a white bow tie and a black tail-coat

A gentleman's residence

Single gentlemen such as Dr Jekyll lived alone in very large houses. They were not expected to look after themselves. Their servants did everything for them, from cooking and cleaning to helping them dress, serving them their food, and answering the door.

Domestic tasks

The essential tasks of cleaning and cooking were all carried out by female servants. Dr Jekyll employed a cook and a housemaid, as well as other domestic servants. Their work was hard and the pay was low, but they had a place to live and a reasonably secure job.

Evening dress

Gentlemen such as Dr Jekyll would change into a formal evening suit for dinner parties, even those with a small group of close friends.

The butler

Both Dr Jekyll and Dr Lanyon were wealthy enough to employ butlers, who managed their households and domestic staff. The butler was the servant who was closest to the master.

STEVENSON'S LONDON

The lives of the rich in London included a busy round of balls, parties, and visits to the theatre. Stevenson, however, concentrates on a small close-knit group of gentlemen who keep themselves to themselves. He does not depict happy, noisy, or crowded scenes. In this book, the sun hardly ever shines and most of the action happens at night.

Lonely atmosphere
The London of the book is a dream-like city dominated by fog, darkness, and the eerie light of the gas lamps used to light the streets in those days.

Ladies and gentlemen leaving the theatre

The other city
A few minutes' walk from Jekyll's luxurious home, lay another London, worlds apart from it. In poor areas, such as Soho, dirty children roamed past ragged washing in the streets, and criminals stalked the night.

Soho: one of the poorest areas of London

Crime and the police
The Metropolitan Police, founded in 1834, had made some progress against crime by the 1880s, but it was still rife in London. Expert pickpockets worked the streets, stealing watches and wallets from the well-to-do.

1880s policemen wore uniforms like this

Fear of crime
There was a great public interest in crime in the 1880s. In 1887, the first Sherlock Holmes story appeared. In 1888, London was transfixed by the gruesome, unsolved murders committed by Jack the Ripper.

Concerned citizens trying to find Jack the Ripper; people from all parts of society came under suspicion.

OXFORD STREET

Rich women (left) enjoyed much luxury but little freedom.

WOMEN IN THE BOOK

There are no major female characters in the book. The main characters are all single men, living in an exclusive, protected male world.

Second-class citizen
Despite the fact that Britain's head of state was a woman, Queen Victoria, women were second-class citizens and could not vote. Wealthy women did not go out to work. They stayed at home, looked after their families, and ran their households.

The dark side of London
Soho was well-known for its music halls, cheap restaurants, and more dubious pleasures. A gentleman would never go to a low-life area such as this. At night, when respectable London was asleep, Soho was busy.

Soho was a centre for crime and many kinds of illegal activities.

Chapter one

THE DOOR

THE TALE I AM ABOUT TO TELL is one of terror and horror such as you may never have heard; a tale to make your flesh creep and your blood run cold. It is a tale of great foolishness and mad ambition, of terrible deeds, and of a creature from the very depths of Hell, who...

But I am ahead of myself. I must begin at the beginning.

My name is Gabriel John Utterson.

I am a lawyer by trade and I like to think that I am respected among my peers,

A lawyer at work
As a lawyer, Utterson was a respected person in society. His work in drawing up wills and contracts brought him into contact with the private lives of many important society figures.

A sinister block of building thrust out onto the street. It was two storeys high, with no window to be seen.

though I know that some consider me a dry old stick.

The chief jewel of each week for me is a Sunday walk with my amiable young cousin Richard Enfield. Others have wondered at our friendship, for indeed we have little in common. But affection, like ivy, grows with time, and is strongest with those of one's own blood, or with old friends. Nothing would induce either of us to miss these Sunday walks.

It was on one of these rambles that we chanced upon a side street in a busy quarter of London. The street drove a thriving trade on weekdays. Even on Sunday, it shone out in contrast to its dingy neighbourhood, like a fire in a forest. With its freshly painted shutters, well-polished brass, and air of cleanliness and gaiety, it instantly caught and pleased the eye of the passerby.

Two doors from one corner, the line was broken by the entrance to a courtyard; and just at that point a sinister block of building thrust out onto the street. It was two storeys high, with no window to be seen, and nothing but a badly neglected door on the lower floor. It bore the marks of prolonged neglect.

My cousin lifted up his cane and pointed.

"Did you ever notice that door?" he asked. "It is connected in my mind with a very odd story."

The Sunday walk
The traditional Sunday walk was a time for gossip, hearsay, and storytelling. On this Sunday, Utterson hears the beginning of a strange story.

"On weekdays"
Streets of shops or market stalls (above) were very busy during the week, and a lifeless, windowless building might not have been noticed.

"The man trampled calmly over the child's body."

Hyde and the family
Mrs Stevenson told her husband Robert to include this incident to emphasize Hyde's brutality. It shocked middle-class Victorian readers who preferred to think of children safe in the parlour at home.

Now as it happened, I knew that door. It was the rear entrance to my friend Henry Jekyll's house.

"It happened like this," Richard began. "I was on my way home at about three o'clock on a black winter morning, and my way lay through a part of town where there was nothing to be seen but lamps – street after street, all lighted up as if for a procession and all as empty as a church. Suddenly, I saw two figures: one a little man who was stumping along at a good pace, the other a girl of maybe eight or ten, running hard down a cross street. Well, these two ran into one another at the corner, but then came the horrible part. The man trampled calmly over the child's body and left her screaming on the ground. It was hellish to see."

"I can imagine," I said.

"I took to my heels," my cousin continued, "collared the gentleman, and brought him back. He was perfectly cool and made no resistance, but he gave me a look so ugly that it brought me out in an icy sweat. Quite a group had gathered round the child by this time – her own family, as it turned out and, pretty soon, the doctor, for whom she had been sent. Now, I had taken a loathing to this gentleman at first sight, so had the child's family, which was only natural after what he'd done. I never saw such hatred on a circle of faces. And there was our man in the middle, with a kind of black, sneering coolness – frightened, too – but carrying it off, sir, really like Satan. 'Now let's avoid a scene,' the man said. 'Name your price.' The family demanded a hundred pounds, which he agreed to pay. The next thing was to get the money, and where do you think he took us, but to that very door. He whipped out a key, went in, and came back with ten pounds in gold and a Coutts's Bank cheque for the balance signed by someone other than himself – someone rather well known about town."

An uneasy feeling had crept over me. "Do you know the name of the man who walked over the child?"

"His name was Hyde," Richard answered. "Mr Edward Hyde."

And now a cold chill gripped my heart. "What does he look like?"

"He's not easy to describe. There is something wrong with his appearance; something displeasing, something downright detestable. I never saw a man I so disliked, and yet I scarce know why. He looked deformed in some way, though what his deformity might have been I cannot say. He's an extraordinary looking man, but I can't describe him. And it's not because I can't remember, I can see him at this moment."

"You say the cheque was not signed by him," I said. "Well then, I believe I know what name was on it, for that door leads into the house of a friend of mine."

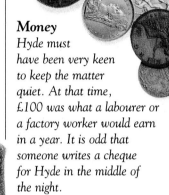

Money
Hyde must have been very keen to keep the matter quiet. At that time, £100 was what a labourer or a factory worker would earn in a year. It is odd that someone writes a cheque for Hyde in the middle of the night.

"I took to my heels and collared the gentleman."

My good cousin started at this, then shifted about with embarrassment. "I think you might have warned me," he said with a touch of sullenness. "Now I'm ashamed of my gossiping tongue. Forgive me, Gabriel. Let us make a bargain never to refer to this again."

"With all my heart," I said, and we shook hands on it.

When we parted my mind was sorely troubled. Hitherto, I had known nothing about Edward Hyde beyond his name. I had not, till now, imagined him a monster.

A 19th-century safe

Safe secret

As Jekyll's lawyer, Utterson is in charge of his will. A will usually comes into effect on death, but Jekyll's will mysteriously includes "disappearance".

Cavendish Square

Situated just to the north of Oxford Street in London's West End, Cavendish Square was one of the most respectable addresses a gentleman could have.

Revolutionary science

Medical knowledge was developing rapidly, thanks to scientists such as Louis Pasteur (below). Lanyon is angered by his friend Jekyll's "unscientific" fancies about what medicine can achieve.

Chapter two

SEARCH FOR MR HYDE

IT HAS LONG BEEN MY CUSTOM after dinner on a Sunday to sit by the fire and read until the church clock rings out the hour of twelve, whereupon I take myself to bed. On this night, however, as soon as my meal was done I went to my business room, where I took from my safe the Last Will and Testament of Dr Henry Jekyll. I sat down to study the document, groaning as I read these words:

I, Henry Jekyll, being of sound mind, do declare that in the event of my death or disappearance all my possessions should pass into the hands of my friend Edward Hyde and that the said Mr Hyde should step into my shoes without delay and take my place as head of my household.

This document had long troubled me. I had from the first thought it madness for Jekyll to leave his fortune, his very substantial fortune, to a man unknown to me. But now, having learnt something of Mr Hyde, I was even more concerned.

Returning the will to my safe I put on my coat and set out for Cavendish Square, where lived my friend, the great Dr Lanyon. If anyone knew about Jekyll, it would be him.

Lanyon's butler ushered me into the dining room, where my friend sat alone over a glass of wine. Lanyon was a hearty, healthy, dapper, red-faced gentleman, with a shock of prematurely white hair and a boisterous and decided manner. We had attended school and college together, and had always thoroughly enjoyed one another's company.

At sight of me Lanyon sprang from his chair and welcomed me with both hands.

After a little rambling talk, I led up to the subject which preoccupied me so. "I suppose, Lanyon, that you and I must be Henry Jekyll's oldest friends … "

He chuckled. "I wish the friends were not quite so old, but yes, I suppose we are. I see little of him now, though."

"Oh?" I said. "I thought you two shared a common interest, both being medical men."

"We did once," Lanyon sighed, "but we haven't been close for more than ten years. He began to go wrong, wrong in mind. Jekyll's head is full of such unscientific balderdash. Far too fanciful."

Ah, I thought, relieved, they've had a falling out only over some scientific matter. "I wonder," I said, "if you've ever come across another, more recent friend of his, one Hyde?"

"Hyde?" repeated Lanyon. "No. Never heard of him."

Old boy network
As though part of a club, wealthy boys would attend an expensive school and then go on to a university, such as Oxford, Cambridge, or Edinburgh. In these exclusive places, firm friendships were formed which lasted for life.

Lanyon sighed, "He began to go wrong, wrong in mind."

And that was all the information I carried home with me. That night I tossed and turned in my great dark bed until the small hours, besieged by uneasy questions and dreams. I saw a great field of lamps in a nocturnal city; the figure of a man walking swiftly; a child running; and then that human monster crushing the child down and passing on regardless of her screams. The figure haunted me all night. And if at any time I slept, it was but to see it glide more stealthily through sleeping houses, or move more swiftly and still more swiftly, even to dizziness, through the maze of streets of a lamplighted city, and at every street corner crush a child and leave her screaming. This fiend had no face, or one

that baffled me and melted before my eyes; and thus it was that
there sprang into my mind a strong curiosity to behold the features
of the real Mr Hyde and see for myself what manner of man he was.
If I could but once set eyes on him, the mystery might lighten and
perhaps roll away, as is the habit of mysterious things when
examined closely. I might see a reason for my friend's strange
preference and for the startling clauses of the will. It would be a face
worth seeing: the face of a man without mercy. A face which had
but to show itself to inspire in people's minds a spirit of enduring
hatred.

I resolved then and there to return to that street of bright shutters
and gleaming brass, and wait there till Hyde once again came to
Jekyll's door. If he's Mr Hyde, I thought boldly, well then, I shall be
Mr Seek.

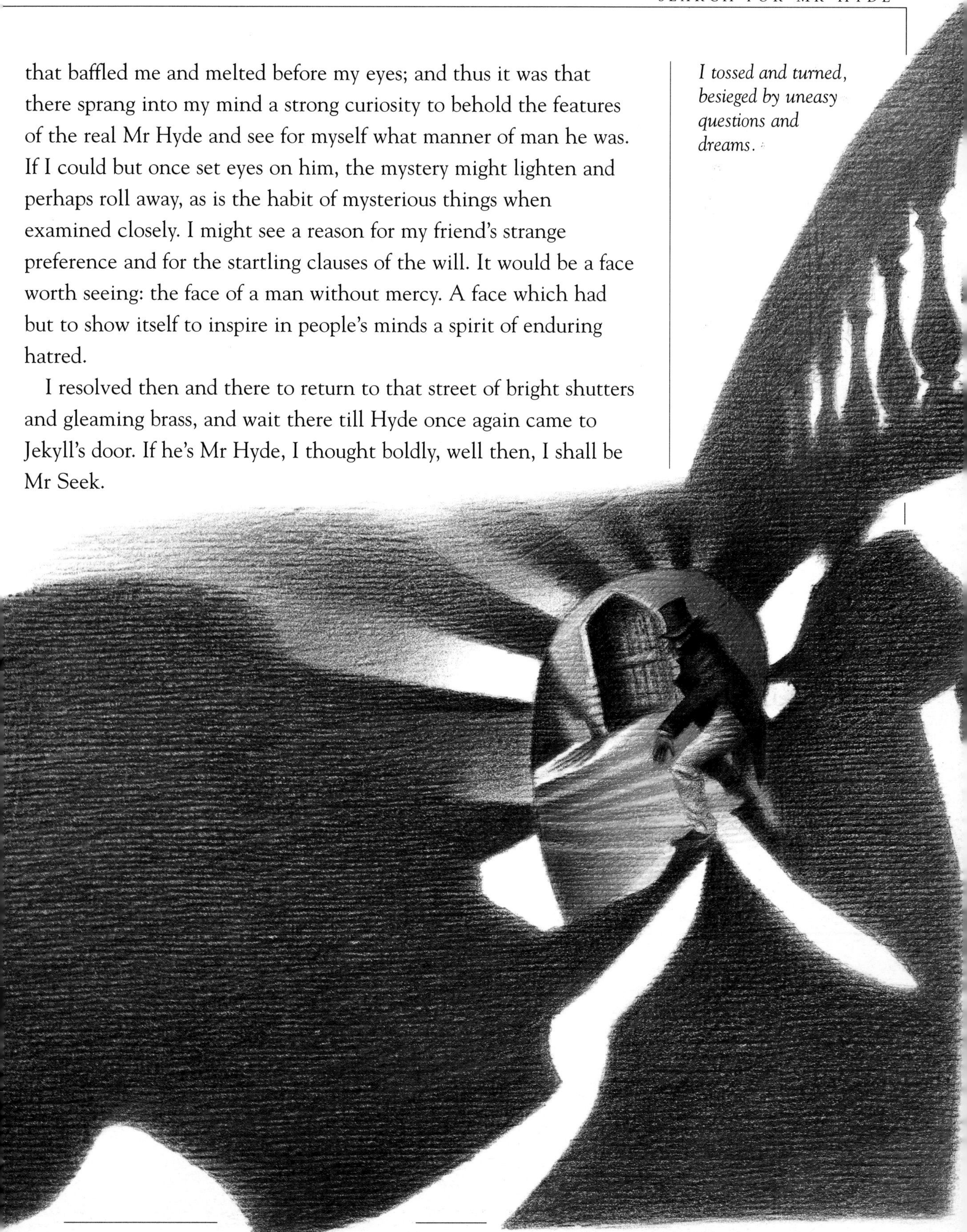

*I tossed and turned,
besieged by uneasy
questions and
dreams.*

Lamps were cleaned and lit at dusk.

Gas street lighting

London's main streets were lit by gas lamps. More than 180 m (200 yd) apart, they gave less light than modern lights. Criminals could take advantage of the dinginess.

Lighting lamps along the Thames Embankment, London.

Key

Edward Hyde has a key to Dr Jekyll's back door. Utterson is keen to find a key to the mystery of their relationship.

I began to haunt the rear entrance of Jekyll's house. In the morning before office hours, at noon when business was plenty and time scarce, at night under the fogged city moon, by all lights, at all hours, I was at my post.

And at last my patience was rewarded. It was a fine dry night with a frost in the air. The street lamps, unshaken by any wind, drew a regular pattern of light and shadow. By ten o'clock the street was solitary and, in spite of the low growl of London from all around, very silent; so silent indeed that I heard the odd, light footsteps long before I saw the one who made them. The steps drew swiftly nearer, and swelled out suddenly louder as they turned the corner. I withdrew into the shadows to observe what manner of man I was to deal with. He was small, and very plainly dressed, and as he made for the door he drew a key from his pocket. I stepped out and touched him on the shoulder.

"Mr Hyde, I think?"

He shrank back with a hissing intake of breath. But his fear was only momentary and, though he did not look me directly in the face, he answered coolly enough.

"That is my name. What do you want?"

"I see you are going inside," I replied. "I am an old friend of Dr Jekyll's – Mr Utterson of Gaunt Street – you must have heard my name. Meeting you so conveniently, I thought you might admit me."

"Dr Jekyll is not at home." He spoke in a husky, whispering, somewhat broken voice. "Now how do you know me?"

"Why, by description. We have friends in common. Henry Jekyll for one."

"He never described me to you. Why are

you lying?" cried Hyde with a flush of anger.

"Come now," I said, "this is not fit language between gentlemen."

At this he gave a savage laugh and lifted his head so that I saw him plainly for the first time. He was pale, with a displeasing smile and a murderous look in his eye. I felt, in an instant, a disgust, loathing, and fear such as I had never known. If ever I read Satan's signature upon a face it was on Mr Edward Hyde's.

"Perhaps it is as well that we've met," he said. "You should have my address."

He gave me a house number and the name of a street in Soho; and then, with extraordinary speed, he unlocked the door and disappeared into the house.

He was small, and very plainly dressed, and as he made for the door he drew a key from his pocket.

The butler greeted guests at the door and took their hats and coats.

The butler
The butler was the senior male servant in a house, and the one who had the most contact with the master.

Household servants
As a wealthy bachelor, Jekyll would have employed six or seven servants.

The front door
A master's friends entered a house through the front door. Back doors were for servants and tradesmen. Hyde, oddly, enters by the back door to the laboratory, or dissecting room.

A large Victorian hallway.

Badly shaken by the encounter, I walked round the corner into a square of ancient, handsome houses. I stopped and knocked at the door to Jekyll's house, which, as ever, wore a great air of wealth and comfort. The door was opened almost at once by the butler.

"Is Dr Jekyll at home, Poole?"

"I will see, Mr Utterson." Poole admitted me and went off to seek his master.

The large comfortable hall, warmed by a bright open fire, was one of my favourite rooms in all of London, but tonight there was a shudder in my blood. The face of Hyde sat heavy on my memory and I seemed to read a menace in the flickering of the firelight on the polished oak cabinets and the uneasy starting of the shadow on the ceiling. I admit, to my shame, a feeling of relief when Poole returned to announce that Dr Jekyll was out.

"Poole," I said, "I saw a gentleman, a Mr Hyde, enter by the old dissecting-room back door some minutes ago. Is that all right when Dr Jekyll is not at home?"

"Quite all right, sir. Mr Hyde has been given a key."

"Your master seems to place a great deal of trust in that young man."

"Yes, sir, he does indeed," answered Poole. "The other servants and I have orders to obey Mr Hyde at all times."

"I do not think I have ever met Mr Hyde here?"

"Oh no, sir. He never *dines* here." replied Poole. "Indeed we see very little of him on this side of the house.

He comes and goes by the laboratory."

I set off for home with a very heavy heart. Poor Harry Jekyll, I thought to myself, what the devil's he got himself into? This Mr Hyde must have secrets of his own, dark secrets compared to which poor Jekyll's worst would be like sunshine. Things cannot continue as they are – if Hyde suspects the existence of the will, he may grow impatient to inherit.

I seemed to read a menace in the flickering of the firelight.

Chapter three

AFTER DINNER AT JEKYLL'S

WHEN I NEXT WENT TO JEKYLL'S it was on a rather more pleasant outing. He had invited half a dozen of his old cronies to dinner, and a splendid time was had by all.

At the end of the evening I contrived to remain behind after the others had departed. Jekyll sat on the opposite side of the fire, a large, well made, smooth-faced man of fifty, with something of a slyish look, but every mark of kindness.

"I've been wanting to speak to you, Jekyll," I began. "You know that will of yours?"

"My poor Utterson, you are unfortunate in such a client. I never saw a man so distressed as you were by my will."

"I can't pretend that I shall ever like him."

"You know I never approved of it."

"Yes, certainly, I know that," said the doctor, a trifle sharply. "You have told me so."

"Well, I tell you so again," I said. "I approve even less now that I've learnt something of young Hyde."

The large handsome face of Henry Jekyll grew pale to the very lips, and a blackness came into his eyes.

"I do not care to hear more," he said.

"What I heard was abominable."

"You do not understand my position, Utterson. It is a very strange one, and it cannot be mended by talking about it."

"But Jekyll, you know me: I am a man to be trusted. Make a clean breast of this in confidence. I am in no doubt I can get you out of it."

"My dear Utterson," replied Jekyll. "This is very good of you, and I cannot find words to thank you. I trust you more than any man alive, but it isn't what you fancy. To put your good heart at rest, I'll tell you one thing; the moment I choose, I can be rid of Mr Hyde. You have my word on that. I will add just one more thing, and I'm sure you'll take it in good part: this is a private matter, and I beg of you to let it sleep."

I reflected a little, looking in the fire. "I have no doubt you are perfectly right," I said at last, getting to my feet.

The doctor continued, "But since we've touched upon this business – and for the last time, I hope – there is one point I should like you to understand. I have a very great interest in poor Hyde. I know you have seen him, he told me so; and I fear he was rude. If I'm taken away suddenly I want you to promise me that you'll get his rights for him. I think you would if you knew all."

"I can't pretend that I shall ever like him," I muttered as we walked to the door.

"I don't ask that," pleaded Jekyll, laying his hand upon my arm. "I only ask for justice, I only ask you to help him for my sake when I am no longer here."

I heaved a great sigh. "I promise."

Gentlemen dining
Jekyll's men-only dinner party is typical of the time. Many men socialized and worked with men rather than women.

Separate lives
Apart from social occasions, the main characters don't share their homes and lives with anyone. They are unmarried, and no one shares their secrets.

Chapter four

THE CAREW MURDER

NEARLY A YEAR LATER, in the month of October, a crime took place – a crime of such ferocity that London was shaken to its very foundations. As it happened, I was one of the first to hear of it. It was early and I was still in bed when my man informed me that I had visitors. I went down to find three policemen awaiting me.

"Are you Gabriel John Utterson, sir?"

"I am, yes."

The sergeant handed me an envelope that bore my name. I opened it as I was bid and read the contents.

"Who's it from?" the sergeant asked.

"A client of mine, Sir Danvers Carew." Sir Danvers was a well-respected member of Parliament, known to all. "Now what's this about? How did this letter come into your possession?"

"It was found on a gentleman who's been murdered, sir. It looks as if he was on his way to post it to you when he was attacked."

"Sir Danvers – murdered?" I cried.

"It may not be him, sir. For all we know, the deceased may have been carrying the letter to the post for Sir Danvers. But perhaps you'd be good enough to come down to the station and take a look at the body."

I dressed in haste and accompanied the policemen to the cell where the body had been carried. It was a terrible sight. The poor man had been beaten to death – by a maniac, it seemed – but there was no doubt of the victim's identity.

On the beat
London's police force had an excellent reputation. They were highly disciplined, and were trained to treat all citizens with respect.

1880s dark blue uniform

Police whistle

Truncheon

Crime at the time
There was much unease about crime in the 1880s. A bishop reported that the cry "murder" was heard once every five minutes in the poorer parts of London.

Houses of Parliament, London

Parliament
There were 670 Members of Parliament (MPs). They were not paid a salary, so had to be rich enough to support themselves. The death of a well-known MP would cause a public outcry.

"Yes," I said, "I recognize him. I am sorry to say that this is Sir Danvers Carew."

"Good God, sir," exclaimed the officer in charge, Inspector Newcomen, "is it possible?" The next moment his eye lighted up. "This will make a deal of noise. Perhaps you can help us to the guilty man."

The inspector went on to tell me that the murder had been witnessed by a maid-servant living alone in a house near the river.

"She had gone upstairs to bed about eleven. The early part of the night was cloudless, and the lane, which the maid's window overlooked, was brilliantly lit by the full moon."

There was no doubt of the victim's identity.

"As she sat down by the window," the Inspector continued, "she noticed an aged, white-haired gentleman strolling along – Sir Danvers Carew as we now know. At the same time she observed, coming from the opposite direction, another gentleman, a small man whom she recognized as one who had once visited her master on some business matter. A very unpleasant, wicked-looking man, so she said, by the name of Mr Edward Hyde."

I quailed at the sound of this name. Hyde again, after all this time!

"When the two men came within speaking distance, Sir Danvers bowed politely and, apparently in no hurry, stopped to chat. It did not seem as if the subject of their conversation was very important; he could have just been asking the way. But the whole time he spoke, the other man – Mr Hyde – fiddled impatiently with his cane as if wishing to be on his way, and answered

"Yes," I said, "I recognize him. I am sorry to say that this is Sir Danvers Carew."

"Good God, sir," exclaimed the officer in charge, Inspector Newcomen, "is it possible?" The next moment his eye lighted up. "This will make a deal of noise. Perhaps you can help us to the guilty man."

The inspector went on to tell me that the murder had been witnessed by a maid-servant living alone in a house near the river.

"She had gone upstairs to bed about eleven. The early part of the night was cloudless, and the lane, which the maid's window overlooked, was brilliantly lit by the full moon."

There was no doubt of the victim's identity.

"As she sat down by the window," the Inspector continued, "she noticed an aged, white-haired gentleman strolling along – Sir Danvers Carew as we now know. At the same time she observed, coming from the opposite direction, another gentleman, a small man whom she recognized as one who had once visited her master on some business matter. A very unpleasant, wicked-looking man, so she said, by the name of Mr Edward Hyde."

I quailed at the sound of this name. Hyde again, after all this time!

"When the two men came within speaking distance, Sir Danvers bowed politely and, apparently in no hurry, stopped to chat. It did not seem as if the subject of their conversation was very important; he could have just been asking the way. But the whole time he spoke, the other man – Mr Hyde – fiddled impatiently with his cane as if wishing to be on his way, and answered never a word. Then, all of a sudden, he broke out in a great flame of anger, stamping his foot and brandishing his cane and carrying on like a madman. The old gentleman – Sir Danvers – took a step back with the air of one very much surprised and a trifle hurt. At that, Mr Hyde went wild and clubbed him to the ground, and next moment, with an apelike fury, he was trampling his victim underfoot, and hailing down a storm of blows, under which the bones were audibly shattered and the body jumped upon the ground. At the horror of these sights and sounds, the maid fainted."

"When did you hear about all this?" I asked the inspector.

"It was about two o'clock when the maid came to and called us in. The murderer was gone long since, but his victim still lay in the lane, incredibly mangled. The stick with which the deed was done, though of some rare and very tough and heavy wood, had snapped in the middle under the pressure of the cruel blows, and one splintered half had rolled into the gutter. Here it is, Mr Utterson, see for yourself."

He placed the broken stick before me, and my mouth went dry, for I knew it well. Broken and battered as it was, I recognized the stick as one I had myself presented many years before to Henry Jekyll.

I made no mention of Jekyll's connection with Hyde, but I saw no reason to protect his heir. "If you will come with me," I said to the Inspector, "I think I can take you to Mr Hyde."

Mr Hyde went wild and clubbed him to the ground.

The dismal quarter of Soho appeared to me like a district of some city in a nightmare.

London fog
The mystery deepens with the fog slowing Utterson's cab. Everyone in London used coal fires for heat, and the smoke produced the famous fog, which could last for months.

Chapter five

MR HYDE'S HOUSE

IT WAS BY THIS TIME about nine in the morning, and the first fog of the season had come down, so that our cab crawled from street to street. The dismal quarter of Soho that we came to, where the fog swirled more densely than ever and the street lamps were still lit, appeared to me like a district of some city in a nightmare.

As the cab drew up before the address Hyde had given me at our brief, unpleasant meeting almost a year before, the fog lifted a little and showed a dingy street, with many ragged children huddled in doorways. So this was the home of Jekyll's favourite; of a man who was heir to a quarter of a million pounds.

The old woman who opened the door had a mean, pale face. "Yes, this is Mr Hyde's," she said, "but he's not at home."

*Newcomen pounced
upon the stick.*

He had, she told us, been in last night very late, but had gone away again in less than an hour. There was nothing strange in this, she said, he was a man of irregular habits and was often away for long periods. It was nearly two months since she had seen him till yesterday. When my companion informed the woman that he was Inspector Newcomen of Scotland Yard, a flash of odious joy appeared on her face.

"Ah!" said she, "he's in trouble then! What has he done?"

Inspector Newcomen and I exchanged glances. "Hyde doesn't seem a very popular character," said Newcomen. "Now let us by to have a look round."

We entered the house of Edward Hyde. The housekeeper lived on the ground floor and Hyde used only a couple of rooms on the floor above. These were furnished with luxury and taste. A closet was filled with fine wines, he used only the best silverware, and the curtains were agreeable in colour. A good picture hung upon one of the walls – a gift, I supposed, from Henry Jekyll who knew much about art.

But however elegant the rooms, at this moment they bore every mark of having been recently and hurriedly ransacked. Clothes lay about the floor, drawers stood open, and on the hearth there lay a pile of grey ashes, as though many papers had been burned. And then, lying behind the door, we found the other half of the stick that had killed Sir Danvers, which Newcomen pounced upon with delight.

"Proof indeed that Hyde's our man! I have him, Mr Utterson! He'll not escape me now!"

*Jekyll handed me
the letter.*

Chapter six

A LETTER FROM MR HYDE

IT WAS LATE in the afternoon by the time I found my way to Jekyll's house. There, I was admitted by Poole, who escorted me through the kitchen and across the courtyard to what was known as the laboratory or the dissecting rooms. At the far end, a flight of stairs rose to the red door of Jekyll's study, where I had never been before. The study was a large room, furnished with cabinets and a desk. A fire burned in the grate; a lighted lamp was set on the mantelpiece, for even in the houses the fog began to lie thickly. And there, close up to the warmth, sat Dr Jekyll, looking deadly sick. He did not rise to meet me but held out a cold hand and bade me welcome in a changed voice.

"And now," I said, as soon as Poole had left us, "have you heard the news?"

"They were crying it in the square," replied Jekyll with a shudder. "I heard it from my dining room."

"Well," I said, "Carew was my client, but so are you. I am in a difficult position and have to know what I'm doing. You haven't been mad enough to hide this fellow?"

"Utterson, I swear to God," cried the doctor, "after this I will never set eyes on Hyde again. I am done with him. It is all at an end. Indeed he does not want my help; you do not know him as I do. And you may mark my words, he'll never be heard of again."

"Well, I hope you're right," I said, "for your sake. If it came to a trial, your name might come up, and think of the scandal then."

"I'm quite sure of him," replied Jekyll. "I have grounds for certainty that I cannot share with anyone. But there is one thing on which you might advise me, Utterson. I have – I have just received a letter and I'm at a loss whether I should show it to the police.

I would like to leave it in your hands. You would judge wisely I am sure; I have great trust in you."

"You fear that it might lead to his detection?" I asked.

"No," replied Jekyll. "I don't care what becomes of Hyde. I was thinking of my own character."

"Let me see the letter," I said.

Jekyll got up and went to his desk. He handed me the letter, which was written in an odd, upright hand. It read as follows:

To Dr Henry Jekyll, my great benefactor,
I have repaid your generosity very poorly. Do not fear for my safety. I have a means of escape on which I can depend. I bid you farewell. Think no more of me, Sir, I do not deserve your charity.
Your servant,
Edward Hyde

Paper boys
Before radio and television, newspapers were the quickest way to spread news. The cries of the paper boys chanting their headlines were the public's first warning of exciting news.

"Have you the envelope?" I asked Jekyll.

"I burned it," replied Jekyll, "before I thought about it. But it bore no postmark. It was delivered by hand."

"I must give this some thought." I slipped the letter into my pocket. "And now, at last, perhaps you can tell me about your will. The wording of the thing – that everything should go to Hyde in the event of your 'death or disappearance' – was it Hyde who dictated that?"

For a moment Jekyll looked quite faint, then he shut his mouth tight and merely nodded.

"I knew it," I said. "He meant to murder you for your money. You've had a fine escape, Jekyll."

"I've had more than an escape," the doctor replied solemnly. "I have learnt a severe lesson. Oh God, Utterson, what a lesson I've had!"

And he covered his face with his hands.

The Evening News & Post
Special Edition OCTOBER 25
SHOCKING MURDER OF AN M.P.

The power of the press
The number of newspapers multiplied in the late 19th century. Thanks to them, a shocking story such as this would reach almost everyone.

Leading lawyers in London had chambers (offices) in Gray's Inn.

Legal work

In their work, Utterson and Guest were used to analysing documents closely. In the privacy of his home, Utterson takes his chief clerk into his confidence.

On the way out I stopped for a word with Jekyll's manservant. "Poole, I believe a letter was brought by messenger earlier. Can you tell me anything about him? His looks, his manner?"

Poole looked puzzled. "If there was a messenger I didn't see him, sir. And I know nothing of any letter."

I left the house. Outside in the square, the news boys were shouting themselves hoarse.

"Special edition! Shocking murder of an MP!"

I could not help my sudden fear that,

Guest compared the two documents.

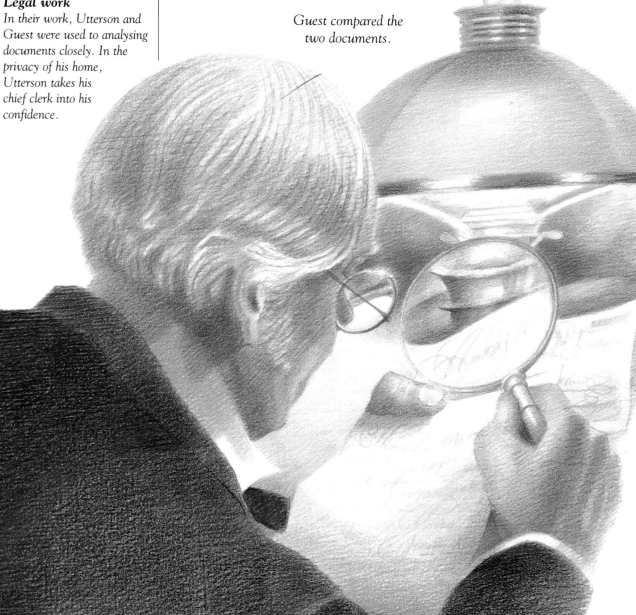

following hard on the heels of the death of one friend and client, another was about to be ruined by scandal.

Back home, my chief clerk, Mr Guest, joined me in a glass of fine old wine by the fireside. Guest had been with me for many years. I trusted him completely and kept few secrets from him. It was in my mind to show him the letter Jekyll had given me and learn something of the writer, for Guest was a great student of handwriting, and claimed to be able to tell much about a man from the slope and flourish of his hand.

"This is a sad business about Sir Danvers," I said to him.

"It is indeed, sir," he replied. "The murderer, of course, was quite mad."

"I should like to hear your views on that," I said. "I have a letter here in his handwriting. This is between ourselves, for I don't know what to do about it; it is an ugly business at best. But here, look it over, tell me what you think."

Guest's eyes brightened, and he took the letter from me and studied it with passion. Very shortly he said, "No, sir, he's not mad. But this is an odd hand."

Just then a servant entered with a note.

"Is that from Dr Jekyll, sir?" inquired Guest. "I thought I knew the writing. Anything private, Mr Utterson?"

"Only an invitation to dinner. Why? Do you want to see it?"

"Just for a moment, thank you, sir."

Guest placed the invitation and the letter side by side. There was a long pause while he compared the two documents.

"What is it?" I said at last, unable to contain myself.

"Well, sir, there's a great resemblance between the two hands. Indeed, in many points they are identical, only differently sloped."

My hand shook as I took the letter from him and folded it. "I'd rather you said nothing of this, Guest – to anyone."

"No, sir. I understand."

No sooner was I alone than I locked the letter in my safe. It seemed that Hyde's note had not been written by him at all, but by Jekyll himself. So my old friend had come to this – forging documents for a murderer! My blood ran cold in my veins.

One hand

As a student of handwriting (graphologist), Guest notices the similarities between Jekyll's and Hyde's writing style. He also concludes the murderer is sane.

Writing styles

Dr Jekyll and Mr Hyde

Wide loops in top parts of letters (ascenders) show the person is emotional.

Tall and thin writing shows caution and restraint.

Dr Jekyll and Mr Hyde

Writing slanting to left often shows a defensive attitude.

Large writing reveals an outgoing personality.

Dr Jekyll and Mr Hyde

Triangular loops reveal desire to control others.

No detail too small

For graphologists, the way a single letter is written can suggest an important aspect of character.

Mr Utterson
Short t-bar: caution

Mr Utterson
Long t-bar: energy

Mr Utterson
Wavy t-bar: light-heartedness

Mr Utterson
Upwards t-bar: enthusiasm

Chapter seven

DR LANYON RECEIVES A SHOCK

THE KILLING OF SIR DANVERS CAREW caused a stir not only in London but throughout the land, and large rewards were offered for the capture of Edward Hyde. But Hyde had disappeared from the face of the earth as though he had never existed. Much about the man's past was discovered, however. Tales were unearthed about his cruelty, his vile life, his strange companions, his violence. Yet of his present whereabouts there was not a whisper. From the time he had left his house in Soho on the morning of the murder, he was simply blotted out.

Now that Hyde's evil influence was gone, a new

life began for Dr Jekyll. His face brightened, he saw his friends again, he entertained, and busied himself with charity work. He even revived his friendship with Lanyon, which I was very glad to see. For more than two months, the doctor was at peace.

But it was not to last.

On the 8th of January, Lanyon and I dined at Jekyll's house. It was a splendid evening, with Jekyll as lively as I had ever seen him, looking from one to the other of us as in the old days when we three were inseparable friends. Yet, on the 12th, when I called on him, his door was shut against me.

"I'm sorry, sir," Poole said to me. "The doctor is unwell and I have orders to admit no one."

I tried again two days later, and the day after that; but each time, I was refused. I became unsettled. It had become my habit to drop in on my friend regularly, and this return to solitude weighed heavy upon my spirits.

Police investigations
After a murder, police would issue a description of the person wanted for the crime. Large rewards were offered for help leading to the arrest of murderers of public figures, like Sir Danvers.

Hyde had disappeared from the face of the earth as though he had never existed.

"I'm sorry, sir," Poole said to me. "The doctor is unwell and I have orders to admit no one."

I decided to visit Lanyon and discuss it with him. There at least I was not denied admittance, but when I entered his house I was shocked at the change that had taken place in my old friend. He had his death warrant written upon his face. His rosy cheeks had grown pale, his flesh had fallen away, and even his fine head of hair seemed to have thinned. But all this was nothing compared to the look in his eye and quality of manner, which spoke of some

The look in his eye spoke of some deep-seated terror of the mind.

deep-seated terror of the mind.

"I have had a shock, Utterson," he said, "from which I fear I shall never recover. It is a question of weeks. I sometimes think if we knew all, we should be glad to die."

"Jekyll is ill too. Have you seen him?"

But Lanyon's face changed, he held up his trembling hand, and he spoke in a loud, unsteady voice.

"I wish to see or hear no more of Doctor Jekyll. I am quite done with that man, and I beg you not to speak of one whom I regard as dead."

"Can't I do anything?" I asked quietly. "We are three very old friends, Lanyon; we shall not live long enough to make others."

"Nothing can be done," Lanyon answered bitterly. "Ask him."

"I would, but he will not see me."

"I'm not surprised at that," was the reply. "Some day, Utterson, after I'm dead, you may learn the right and wrong of this, but I cannot tell you. Now, let us talk of other things."

When I got home I sat down and wrote to Jekyll, complaining of my exclusion from his house, and asking the cause of this unhappy break with Lanyon. The next day brought an answer, sometimes mysterious:

I do not blame our old friend Lanyon for not wanting to hear of me again, but I share his view that we must never meet. From this day on, I mean to lead a life of extreme seclusion. You must not be surprised, nor doubt my friendship, if my door is often shut even to you. You must suffer me to go my own dark way. I have brought on myself a punishment and a danger that I cannot name. Please respect my silence.

I was amazed to read this. The dark influence of Hyde had been withdrawn, and yet, once again, Jekyll seemed to have been brought down by something worse than madness.

And Lanyon, too. A week after my visit, he took to his bed for the last time. Within a few days he was dead.

Lanyon as he was
Doctor Lanyon had always been a healthy, robust man. There is no physical cause for his sudden loss of health.

Wasting away
Despite Dr Lanyon's scientific background, he has been made ill by an unspeakable terror. It was an accepted feature of Victorian novels that people could die from emotional causes, such as heartbreak or fright.

A grave situation
Lanyon takes the secret of Jekyll and Hyde to his grave. Hyde has killed Sir Danvers, now Lanyon is killed by the shock Jekyll has given him.

PRIVATE: For the eyes of G. J. Utterson ALONE.
To be opened only upon the death or disappearance of Dr Henry Jekyll.

The letter from Dr Lanyon

I received an unexpected visit from Jekyll's butler.

Chapter eight

THE LAST NIGHT

THE NIGHT AFTER Lanyon's funeral, I sat by the light of a melancholy candle turning over an envelope that had been delivered to me shortly after my friend's death. "PRIVATE : For the eyes of G. J. Utterson ALONE," the envelope read in Lanyon's handwriting. "To be opened only upon the death or disappearance of Dr Henry Jekyll." That word again, "disappearance", as in Jekyll's mad will. What could it mean? A great curiosity overcame me, but I could not disregard Lanyon's wishes, and placed the letter in my safe.

One evening after dinner, I received an unexpected visit from Jekyll's butler, who looked frighteningly pale and distracted.

"Bless me, Poole, what ails you? Is the doctor ill?"

"I'm sorry to disturb you, sir," he replied, "but I don't know who else to turn to. There's something wrong at the house. Something badly wrong."

I invited him to sit down, have a glass of wine, and tell me what it was that worried him.

"It's the doctor, sir. He's been shut up in his study across the courtyard for days, and I tell you plain, I'm mortally afraid. I believe there's been foul play."

An icy hand settled on my heart. "Foul play? What kind of foul play?"

"I daren't say, sir," was the answer, "but will you come along with me and see for yourself?"

I went at once for my hat and coat, and we stepped outside.

It was a wild, cold night, with a pale moon. The square, when we got there, was full of wind and dust, and the trees in the garden were lashing themselves along the railing.

"Well, here we are, sir," Poole said, his voice harsh and broken, "and may God grant there be nothing wrong after all."

He knocked on the door to Jekyll's house.

"Is that you, Poole?" a nervous voice asked from within.

"It's all right," said Poole. "Open the door."

The hall, when we entered, was brightly lit, the fire was built high, and about the hearth all of the servants stood huddled together like a flock of sheep. At sight of me, the housemaid started crying, and the cook cried out, "Bless you for coming, Mr Utterson, oh bless you, sir."

The servants stood huddled together like a flock of sheep.

Poole took me through the house, into the courtyard.

Medical drugs
Drugs strong enough to change people's personalities were widely available from chemists. These included opium, which was given in small doses to calm children.

Poole ordered them to be silent, and took me through the house, into the courtyard. We passed through the laboratory, with its crates and bottles, and at the foot of the stairs to Jekyll's study, he motioned me to remain there and listen hard, then mounted the steps and knocked on the red study door.

"Mr Utterson is here, sir," he called, "and asking to see you."

A voice answered from within, an odd, strangled voice: "Tell him I cannot see anyone."

"Thank you, sir," said Poole. Taking his candle, he led me back across the yard into the great kitchen.

"Mr Utterson," he said, "tell me plain, was that my master's voice?"

"It did seem … much changed," I replied cautiously.

"Changed!" Poole cried. "Have I been twenty years in the doctor's house not to know his voice? No, sir, it's my belief that my master's been done away with. And who's in there instead of him, and why does it stay there?"

"This is wild talk," I said. "If Dr Jekyll had been murdered, why would the murderer stay behind? No, no, that doesn't make sense."

"You are a hard man to satisfy, sir," said Poole, "but there's more. All this last week he, or it, or whatever it is that lives in the study, has been crying out night and day for some sort of medicine. He leaves notes for me, sometimes two or three a day, asking for some sort of medicine, a kind of white salt. I've been sent to every chemist in town, sir. Every time I bring the stuff back there's soon another note telling me to return it because it was not pure, and another order for a different firm. That drug is wanted very badly, sir, whatever its purpose."

"And you've not seen your master for some days?" I said.

"Not until this afternoon, and it was that sight of him that drove me to you. I came suddenly into the laboratory from the garden. There he was, at the far end of the room, digging among the crates. When he saw me he gave a cry like a startled rat, and flew past me and up the stairs into the study. I saw him but for a moment, sir, but I tell you, the sight made the hair stand up on my head."

"But what was so frightening about him?" I asked.

"Sir," Poole said, and leaned towards me. "He wore a mask."

"A mask!"

"Now I ask you, sir, if that was my master why would he cover his face? Why would he cry out at the sight of me – me, of all people – and scamper from me like a frightened animal?"

"That drug is wanted very badly, sir, whatever its purpose."

Poker
Heavy iron pokers were used for adjusting the coal fires used for heating.

Axe
Axes were used for chopping wood for the fire. Like pokers, axes made good weapons.

A gentleman's study
Every educated gentleman had a study where he could read a book, write letters, or just relax. Unusually, Jekyll's study and laboratory are separate from his house. No one knows what he does there.

"That is very strange behaviour," I agreed, "but perhaps there is an explanation. God forbid, but your master may have developed some disease that has altered the shape of his face and coarsened his voice. Hence the mask and his wish not to be seen, and his eagerness to find the drug that will cure him."

Poole turned pale. "Sir, that thing was not my master. Dr Jekyll is a tall, fine build of a man, and this was more of a dwarf."

I began to protest. "Oh, sir," cried Poole, "do you think I do not know my master after twenty years? God knows what that thing was, but it was never Dr Jekyll. No, I stand by my claim that there was murder done."

"If you truly believe that," I said, "it becomes my duty to make certain. We must get to the truth of this, even if it means breaking the door down."

Poole's face flushed with excitement. "Now you're talking, sir! There's an axe in the laboratory. I'll take that, and you might take the kitchen poker for yourself."

I seized the poker and balanced it in my hand. "And now comes the question," I said. "Who is going to do it?"

"Why, you and me, sir," Poole replied.

"Let us be plain about this, Poole. I believe that we both think more than we have said. This man you saw – in spite of the mask did you recognize him?"

"Well, sir, he went by so quick, and he was so doubled up that I could hardly swear to it, but if you mean was it Mr Hyde, why yes, I think it was."

"My fear exactly," I said. "Evil, I fear – evil was sure to come of that connection. And if it was Hyde you saw, I think you may be right and poor Harry has been killed, and his murderer still lurks up there in that room. Well, let our name be vengeance. Come! To work!"

Again we went out into the yard. A cloud now stood across the moon, and the wind tossed the light of the candle to and fro, sending our shadows shivering about us. As I led the way up the stairs to Jekyll's study my heart thumped in fear of the evil that might await us behind that door.

As I led the way up
the stairs to
Jekyll's study
my heart
thumped
in fear.

43

There lay the study in the quiet lamplight, a good fire glowing and chattering on the hearth.

At the top of the stairs we pressed our ears to the door, and heard an odd footfall moving slowly back and forth. "So he will walk all day," Poole whispered, "aye, and the better part of the night. Here they come again, a little closer. Mr Utterson, tell me, is that the doctor's foot?"

The steps fell lightly, different indeed to the heavy creaking tread of Henry Jekyll.

"Once, I heard him weeping!" said Poole.

"Weeping?" I asked, feeling a sudden chill of horror.

"Weeping like a lost soul," replied Poole. "A terrible sound. I came away with that upon my heart."

"Well, let's get to the bottom of this," I said, and cried out, "Jekyll, I demand to see you!" The footsteps stopped but there came no reply. "I give you fair warning," I continued, "I must and shall see you. If not by fair means, then by foul – if not of your consent then by brute force!"

And then we heard it, a harsh, shrieking, pathetic voice. "Utterson, for God's sake, have mercy!"

"That's not Jekyll's voice – it's Hyde's!" I cried. "Down with the door, Poole!"

Poole swung the axe over his shoulder; the blow shook the building, and the door leaped against the lock and hinges. A dismal screech of animal terror rang from the study. Up went the axe again, and again it fell upon the sturdy panels. Four times the blow fell, but the wood was tough, the

door well-made, and
it was not until the
fifth that the lock burst and the ruined
door fell inwards.

Then all was still. We stood in the
doorway, and peered in. There lay the
study in the quiet lamplight, a good fire
glowing and chattering on the hearth,
the kettle coming to the boil, papers
neatly set out on the table, and nearer
the fire, the things laid out for tea.
The quietest room, you would
have said, and, if it weren't for the
glazed presses full of chemicals, the
most commonplace in London.

Right in the middle of the room lay the
body of a man sorely contorted and still
twitching.

Poole and I drew near on tiptoe, turned the
body on its back, and beheld the face of Edward
Hyde. He was dressed in clothes far too large
for him; the muscles of his face still moved as
if he were alive, but his life was quite gone.
The crushed vial in his hand, and the
strong odour that hung upon the air, told
me that he had taken his own life.

"We have come too late, either to
save or punish," I said to Poole. "Mr
Hyde is dead. It only remains for us to
find the body of your master."

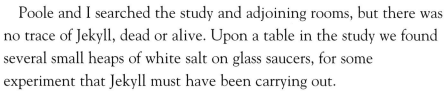

"This glass has seen some strange things," whispered Poole.

Poole and I searched the study and adjoining rooms, but there was no trace of Jekyll, dead or alive. Upon a table in the study we found several small heaps of white salt on glass saucers, for some experiment that Jekyll must have been carrying out.

"This looks like the salt I was always bringing him," said Poole. As he spoke, the kettle boiled over with a startling noise.

This brought us to the fireside, where an easy chair was drawn cosily up. We looked around some more and came to a looking glass, into whose depths we gazed with horror. It was so turned to show us nothing but the rosy glow playing on the roof, the fire sparkling in a hundred repetitions along the glazed front of the presses, and our own pale faces stooping to look in.

"This glass has seen some strange things," whispered Poole.

"And surely none stranger than itself," I said. "For what did Jekyll want with it?"

Next we turned to the desk. Among a neat array of papers, we found a large envelope bearing my name. It contained three enclosures. The first was a new will, drawn up by Jekyll in the same terms as its predecessor, except that in place of the name of Edward Hyde, I read, to my amazement, the name Gabriel John Utterson. "My head goes round," I said. "Hyde must have raged to see himself displaced, and yet he has not destroyed this new will."

The next paper was a note from Jekyll with today's date at the top. "Poole," I cried, "he was alive and here today! Surely he can't have been disposed of in so short a time. He must be still alive, he must have fled."

"Why don't you read it, sir?" Poole said.

"Because I am afraid," I replied. "God grant I have no cause." I then began to read:

My Dear Utterson,
When this falls into your hands I shall have disappeared, under what circumstances I cannot at this time foresee, but of one thing I am certain: the end is very near. Go now, and first read Lanyon's

letter, which he warned me would be placed in your hands following his death. Then, if you care to hear more, turn to the confession of
Your unworthy and unhappy friend,
Henry Jekyll.

My hand fell on a bulky packet sealed in several places, which I put in my pocket. "I would say nothing of this document, Poole. If your master is dead we may at least save his good name. It is now ten. I must go home and read these papers, but I shall be back before midnight, when we'll send for the police."

I trudged home with a heavy heart. In my business room I removed Lanyon's letter from my safe and settled down to read first his narrative, then Jekyll's, knowing, with dreaded certainty, that this mystery was at last to be explained.

PRIVATE: *For the eyes of G. J. Utterson ALONE.*

To be opened only upon the death or disappearance of Dr Henry Jekyll.

I could now read Lanyon's letter.

Chapter nine

LANYON'S LETTER

"ON THE NINTH OF JANUARY, four days ago now," Lanyon's letter began, "I received by the evening delivery an envelope from Henry Jekyll. I was surprised by this, for we had dined together just the night before and I could think of nothing that had not been said then. The contents of the letter increased my wonder, for in it he asked me to cancel any arrangements and go at once to his house. Poole had instructions to take me to Jekyll's study, where I should

remove a certain drawer with all its contents, breaking the lock if necessary. I was then to take the drawer back to Cavendish Square and await the arrival at midnight of a young man, into whose hands I was to place the drawer. He said that his life, his honour, his reason depended on it.

"Reading this I decided that Jekyll must be insane, but for the sake of our old friendship I did as he requested. I went to his house, collected the drawer with Poole's help, and returned home. There, examining the drawer's contents, I found a number of small packages containing white powders of some sort, and a vial half-full of a blood-red liquid. There was also a book full of dates and brief notes, the word "double" appearing several times. There was also the record of a series of experiments.

"There was a policeman not far off and at sight of him my visitor made great haste to come in."

Glass flask

Mysterious chemicals
The mixture that Hyde produces is a mystery. We do not know which chemicals are used.

"At the stroke of midnight the knocker sounded very gently on the door. I went myself to answer the summons, having sent the servants to bed, and found a small figure crouching against the pillars of the porch.

"'Have you come from Dr Jekyll?' I asked.

"He said that he had, and when I bid him enter he cast a backward glance into the darkness. There was a policeman not far off and at sight of him my visitor made great haste to come in. I escorted him to the bright light of my consulting room, where I had my first chance to see him clearly. He was small, as I have said, and his clothes, which were far too big for him, hung loosely about him. I was struck with the shocking expression of his face. There was something abnormal about it, something surprising and revolting. He seemed agitated, afire with a deadly serious excitement.

"'Have you got it?' he cried. So lively was his impatience, he laid his hand upon my arm. I stood back, conscious of an icy pang along my blood.

"'There it is, sir,' I replied, pointing to it on the floor.

"He sprang to it eagerly, and then paused, and laid his hand upon his heart. I could hear his teeth grate, and his face was so ghastly I grew alarmed. 'I'll need a measuring glass,' he said over his shoulder.

"I gave him the glass and he measured out a small amount of the red liquid and added one of the powders. The resultant mixture, at first of a reddish hue, began to brighten in

colour and effervesce audibly. Then the bubbling ceased
and the compound changed briefly to a dark purple before
fading to a watery green. My visitor, who had been
watching these changes keenly, set down the glass and
turned his gaze on me.

"'If you wish it,' he said, 'I'll leave you now and you will
be none the wiser about any of this. But if your curiosity
has the better of you, you might witness
something that will open to you a new
province of knowledge and new avenues to
fame and power. Think carefully, for you
may not like what you see.'"

*He mixed the liquid in
front of Dr Lanyon.*

"'Sir,' said I, affecting a coolness that I did not feel, 'I have gone too far tonight in unexplained services to withdraw before I see the end.'

"'Well said,' he answered. 'But Lanyon, I must bind you to secrecy. And now you who has been bound to the most narrow views – behold.'

"He put the glass to his lips and drank at one gulp. A cry followed. He reeled, staggered, clutched at the table, and held on, staring with injected eyes, gasping with open mouth. And as I looked, there came, I thought, a change – he seemed to swell, his face became suddenly black and the features seemed to melt and alter. The next moment, I sprang to my feet and flew back against the wall, my arm raised to shield me, my mind in terror.

"'Oh God!' I screamed, and again, 'Oh God!'; for there before my eyes – pale and shaken, and half-fainting, and

groping before him with his hands, like a man restored from death – there stood Henry Jekyll.

"What Jekyll told me in the next hour I cannot bring myself to set on paper. I saw what I saw, heard what I heard, and my soul sickened at it. And yet, now that the sight has faded from my eyes, I ask myself if I believe it, and I cannot answer. My life is shaken to its roots. Sleep has left me and the deadliest terror sits by me at all hours of the day and night. My days are surely numbered, for no man can live long after witnessing such things. I cannot even in memory dwell on it without a start of horror. I will say but one thing, Utterson, and that will be more than enough. The creature who crept into my house that night was, on Jekyll's own confession, known by the name of Hyde and hunted in every corner of the land as the murderer of Sir Danvers Carew."

"His features seemed to melt and alter."

PRIVATE
Mr G. J. Utterson

Utterson does as Jekyll had requested, reading Lanyon's letter before he reads Jekyll's "confession".

Chapter ten

JEKYLL'S STATEMENT

SO JEKYLL AND HYDE had been one and the same! A practical, methodical, well-meaning fellow all my life, I no longer knew what to make of anything. I felt my life to be quite ruined. With a trembling hand, I turned to Jekyll's statement.

Jekyll began with an account of his early years, telling how his worst fault had been an impatient love of pleasure, which he found hard to reconcile with the desire to carry his head high and appear grave in public. He had therefore concealed his pleasures; he had lived two lives. To friends such as Lanyon and I he was a decent, honourable chap, but to others not of our acquaintance he was a gadabout, a rake, a rowdy fellow who loved excitement and would sally forth under cover of darkness and indulge in all manner of low acts not suited to a gentleman.

"Both sides of me were in deadly earnest," he wrote. "As the respectable doctor I did not shirk my responsibilities and only ever sought to do good, while as the Jekyll of the night I was equally dedicated to the pursuit of pleasure. With every day I drew steadily nearer the truth: that man is not truly one, but truly two. As I grew older I began to daydream about the possibility of separating my two selves. If each, I told myself, could be housed in separate identities, life would be so much easier. The good could keep steadfastly to the responsible, steady path, the other could go his own way, delivered from the guilt and fear of disgrace of his more upright twin.

"It chanced that my scientific studies suggested that such a miracle was possible, but I hesitated long before I put this theory to the test. I knew I risked death. The temptation of such a discovery at last overcame my alarm. I persevered, until one accursed night I added to a prepared compound a large quantity of a particular salt purchased from a firm of wholesale chemists. I watched this new concoction boil and smoke in the glass, and when it had settled, with a strong glow of

"I began to daydream about separating my two selves."

courage, I drank the potion. A terrible agony followed, a grinding in the bones, a deadly nausea, and a horror of the spirit. But all this passed and then I felt something strange within me, something quite new and incredibly sweet. I felt younger, lighter, and quite wicked, ten times more wicked. I stretched out my hands, and saw hair growing thickly upon them, I ran to the mirror in clothes suddenly too big for me and saw for the first time the appearance of Edward Hyde. The evil side to my nature was less robust and well developed than the good. Hyde was smaller, slighter and younger than Jekyll. As good shone in the face of one, evil was written broadly and plainly on the face of the other and left an imprint of deformity and decay. And yet when I looked upon that ugliness I felt a leap of welcome. This, too, was myself.

"With a strong glow of courage, I drank the potion."

"I did not linger at the mirror. The second part of my experiment had yet to be attempted. I had to see if I had lost my identity completely, or if I could be changed back to my true self by taking the drug again. I swallowed a second draught and experienced the same agonies as before; but soon, to my considerable relief, I was my usual self. Now I had two characters and appearances. One was wholly evil, the other good old Henry Jekyll."

From that time forward, all Jekyll had to do to change from the famous professor into Edward Hyde was to mix the potion and drink it. He made preparations with great care. He took a house for Hyde in Soho, engaging a housekeeper to look after it. In addition he told his servants that Hyde must be allowed to come and go as he pleased. He drew up the will to which I so objected, so that if anything happened to him as Jekyll he could inherit all his money as Hyde.

In the hands of Edward Hyde, Jekyll's pleasures became monstrous. But Jekyll let his conscience sleep. It was Hyde that was guilty. It was Hyde alone that trampled over the child in the street and ran on without a thought. And then:

"Two months before the murder of Sir Danvers, a dreadful thing occurred. I woke with a start, feeling that something was wrong. I looked about me. Then I saw my hand on the bedcover. It was not at all like my broad smooth hand, but thin and knuckly, of a dusky pallor, and covered in thick hair. It was the hand of Edward Hyde. Terror woke up in my breast. I bounded from my bed and rushed to the mirror. At the sight that met my eyes, my blood was changed into something very thin and icy. I had gone to bed as Henry Jekyll and awakened as Edward Hyde – without taking the drug! How was this to be explained?

"I crept through the house and to my study, where I mixed my potion and once again became myself. At breakfast I began to reflect more seriously on my double existence. I spied a danger that the balance of my nature might be permanently overthrown. I would lose the power to change voluntarily and become forever Edward Hyde. I was slowly losing hold of my original and better self, and was becoming my second and worse. Between these two, I felt I had to choose. As so many do, I chose the better part and lacked the strength to keep to it.

"Yes, I preferred the elderly and discontented doctor, surrounded by friends, and cherishing honest hopes. I bade farewell to the liberty, the comparative youth, the secret pleasures I had enjoyed in the disguise of Hyde."

Jekyll resolved never again to take the drug,

In the hands of Edward Hyde, Jekyll's pleasures became monstrous.

though he did not destroy Hyde's clothes or give up the Soho house.

For two full months Jekyll held to his resolve. But time lessened his alarm, and he began to be tortured with longing, as though Hyde were struggling for freedom. At last, in an hour of weakness Jekyll once again made and swallowed the potion.

"My devil had been long caged, and came out roaring. It was on this night that I encountered the unfortunate Carew. That amiable gentleman had merely stopped to pass the time, but I was in no mood for idle chatter. I struck him down and mauled the unresisting body, tasting delight with every blow. It was not till I had begun to weary, that I was suddenly struck through the heart by a cold thrill of terror. A mist cleared, and I realized that my life would be over if the crime were ever laid at my door. I ran to my house in Soho and removed all evidence of Hyde's link with Jekyll (overlooking the top half of the broken cane). Then I set out through the lamplit streets, gloating on my crime.

"Hyde had a song upon his lips as he mixed the potion and raised the glass in toast to his victim. The pangs of transformation had not finished tearing him, before Henry Jekyll fell to his knees in remorse and horror for the night's misdeeds. I tried with tears and prayers to smother the crowd of hideous images and sounds with which my memory swarmed. Then tears of gratitude fell from my eyes. I realized that Hyde could never be again. I was confined to the better part of my existence, and how I rejoiced! I locked the door by which Hyde had come and gone, and ground the key under my heel!"

The next day Jekyll heard that the crime had been witnessed, and the murderer was identified as Edward Hyde. Jekyll was safe, but if Hyde peeped out for an instant the hands of all men would be raised to slay him. Months passed, and Jekyll tried to make up for his crimes, working for the sick, renewing lapsed friendships, enjoying the safety and predictability of ordinary life more than ever.

Jekyll enjoyed the safety and predictability of ordinary life more than ever.

From that night onward, Jekyll was never safe. At any hour, he might become Hyde with barely a shudder's warning.

But it was not to last:

"One fine clear January day I sat quietly on a bench in Regent's Park, thinking how much better I now was than other men. At that moment, a horrible nausea came over me, a deadly shuddering. These sensations passed away and left me faint, but as the faintness too subsided I became aware of a change in my way of thinking, a greater boldness, a contempt of danger. I looked down. My clothes hung formlessly on my shrunken limbs. The hand on my knee was corded and hairy. A moment before I had been wealthy and beloved; and now I was hunted, houseless, a known murderer!

"My reason wavered, but it did not fail me entirely. Hyde rose to the occasion. I could not change back to Jekyll without my potion, but I no longer had a key for the back door – and I could hardly enter by the front as Hyde, for Poole would alert the police. I needed help, and thought of Lanyon.

"I went to a small hotel. Hyde in danger of his life was a new creature to me: shaken with anger, lusting to inflict pain. Yet he mastered his fury and wrote two notes, one to Lanyon, the other to Poole, instructing them about the drawer.

"Then he sat all day in a private room, gnawing his nails, alone with his fears. At nightfall, he set forth in a closed cab and drove about the streets of London. He, I say – I cannot write of him as I. That child of Hell had nothing human; nothing lived in him but fear and hatred. And when at last the driver had begun to grow suspicious, Hyde set out on foot in his misfitting clothes. He walked fast, hunted by his fears, chattering to himself, skulking through the less frequented streets, counting the minutes until midnight when it was time to go to Lanyon's."

Once there, he took the potion and changed back into Jekyll – a sight which was to cost Lanyon his life.

"When I came to myself at Lanyon's, the horror of my old friend affected me somewhat. A change had come over me. I was no longer afraid of the scaffold; it was the horror of being Hyde that tortured me!"

From that night onward, Jekyll was never safe. It was only under the immediate effect of the drug, or even a double dose of the drug, that he could remain Jekyll. At any hour, he might become Hyde with barely a shudder's warning – the pangs of transformation were daily less marked. If he went to bed, or even dozed in his chair, he would awake as that evil being, eager to be off to commit some new atrocity. As Jekyll grew weak from trying not to sleep, a creature eaten up and emptied by fever, the powers of Hyde seemed to grow.

"And then my original supply of the salt that changed me to and from Hyde began to run low. I sent out for more but it did not have the right effect. Each time Poole returned with a new powder the result was the same: it made me ill but did not change me. I was forced to conclude that my first supply had not been pure, and that it was that unknown impurity which was the vital ingredient.

"I finish this statement under the influence of the last of the old powders. This, then, is the last time that Henry Jekyll can think his own thoughts or see his own face in the glass. Nor must I delay too long to finish this, for if Hyde found it he would tear it to pieces. Half an hour from now, when I shall again become that hated personality, and this time forever, all will be lost. Will Hyde die upon the scaffold? Or will he find the courage to commit suicide? God knows; I do not care. This is my true hour of death, and what follows concerns another than myself.

"Here, then, as I lay down my pen and seal up my confession, I bring the life of that unhappy man, Henry Jekyll, to an end."

Death on the scaffold
At that time, the punishment for murder was death by hanging. Executions took place on a raised wooden platform called a scaffold.

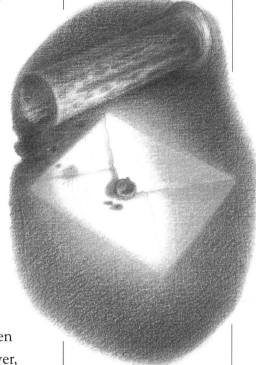

Two deaths
When Jekyll says his life is at an end, he means his life as Jekyll. He will soon turn into Hyde, who commits suicide. In a sense he dies twice, as Jekyll and as Hyde.

THE AUTHOR AND THE BOOK

Jekyll and Hyde reflect the deep divisions in their author's mind. As Stevenson grew up, he was torn between the dutiful, respectable, Christian values of his parents and his own fierce, rebellious spirit. This conflict left him with a strong sense that human nature is divided into two distinct parts, forever at war. When he created Dr Jekyll and Mr Hyde, he finally found the perfect way of expressing this idea.

Mr Hyde kills Sir Danvers

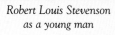

Robert Louis Stevenson as a young man

THE AUTHOR'S EARLY LIFE

Robert Louis Stevenson, often known as "RLS", was born in Edinburgh in 1850, into a prosperous family. As a child he was often ill, and spent much time in bed reading stories. He went to university to study engineering, then switched to law, finally deciding to become a writer instead.

Stevenson's father

Stevenson's father, Thomas Stevenson, was a forceful man and a famous engineer, renowned for his work building harbours and lighthouses. He was a respectable, successful man – a bit like Dr Jekyll. His son chose a wilder path that was less respectable – a little like Mr Hyde. In the original book, Jekyll says that he is like a father, and Hyde like a rebellious son.

RLS's father, Thomas Stevenson

Good and evil

Stevenson had a strict Christian upbringing. He grew up feeling a clear division between good and evil, very aware of the power of evil to destroy, if it is given a chance – as it is by Jekyll.

Scene from a Scottish church

Deacon Brodie

As a child, Stevenson was fascinated by the story of Deacon Brodie, who was a respectable cabinet-maker by day and a robber by night. He had a cabinet made by Brodie in his room, and he even wrote a play about him. Stevenson continued to be fascinated by "doubleness". It is a theme in several of the books he loved, and in several of his own.

The hanging of Deacon Brodie

Although Dr Jekyll and Mr Hyde is set in London, its atmosphere is very reminiscent of the Edinburgh of Stevenson's youth.

The Old Town

As a student, RLS enjoyed the nightlife of Edinburgh's seedy Old Town, shaking off the strict morals of his parents. Sometimes he adopted a complete false identity for his trips into this different world, a strange parallel of Jekyll and Hyde.

The New Town

Stevenson was brought up in Heriot Row in Edinburgh's 18th-century New Town, the smart part of the city. The difference between the New Town and the Old Town resembles that between Jekyll's world and Hyde's.

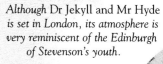

The Old Town

The New Town

The writing of the book

After leaving university, Stevenson worked as a writer. He travelled widely both in Europe and America, both for experience and because of his poor health – his lungs were diseased and he was often ill. From 1884 to 1887 he and his wife lived in Bournemouth, a very quiet and respectable town on the south coast of England. *Dr Jekyll and Mr Hyde* was written there in 1885.

The house in Bournemouth where the Stevensons lived

The story of the dream

Stevenson said that the idea for *Dr Jekyll and Mr Hyde* came to him in a dream. According to his stepson, he wrote the first draft of the book in three days. His wife criticized it, so he burnt it, then wrote another version, the one we have today, in another three days. He revised it during September and October, 1885. It was published in January, 1886, as a cheap "shilling shocker", and was a huge success.

John Singer Sargent painted Stevenson and his wife in 1885.

Mr and Mrs Stevenson

RLS met his wife Fanny in France in 1876, and they were married in San Francisco, USA, in 1880. She had two children from a previous marriage. They lived in the USA, Scotland, Switzerland, France, England (where *Dr Jekyll and Mr Hyde* was written), and finally on the island of Samoa in the South Pacific.

A scene from Kidnapped

STEVENSON'S BOOKS

Stevenson wrote more than 30 books: novels, travel diaries, plays, and collections of stories and essays, some of them in collaboration with other people. His first full-length novel, *Treasure Island* (1883), brought him fame, which increased with the publication of *Dr Jekyll and Mr Hyde* three years later. Among his other well-known books are *Kidnapped* (1886) and its sequel *Catriona* (1893).

A scene from a 1930s edition of Dr Jekyll and Mr Hyde

The great storyteller

When, towards the end of his life, Stevenson settled in Samoa in the South Pacific, he was known there as *Tusitala*, "The Teller of Tales". Because of their gripping storylines, strong characters, brilliant description, and exciting historical settings, many of his books are still widely read today.

The famous character Long John Silver from Treasure Island.

Illustration of the treasure map of Treasure Island

THE LEGEND

D r Jekyll and Mr Hyde have fascinated their readers for more than a century, and have starred many times on stage and screen. They have even become a part of our language: when someone has very separate good and bad sides to their nature, we say they have a "Jekyll and Hyde personality". Stevenson's story has a frighteningly universal appeal; somehow we can all understand how one person can be both Jekyll and Hyde.

Poster for the 1941 film version of Dr Jekyll and Mr Hyde

Good and evil
In this story, the age-old struggle between good and evil takes on a new twist. Dr Jekyll is a mixture of good and evil, but Stevenson said that Jekyll's hypocrisy "let out the beast Hyde … who is the essence of cruelty and malice, and selfishness".

Angels are sometimes taken to represent the good side of human nature.

Devils, or the Devil, can represent the dark side of human nature.

SCIENCE AND FICTION
As well as being a thriller, a detective story, and a horror story, Dr Jekyll and Mr Hyde drew on and anticipated the world of science. It made use of the popular belief that science could do anything.

Ape-like Hyde
In 1859, Charles Darwin had suggested that humans had evolved from apes. Stevenson has Jekyll become the "ape-like" Hyde, who moves "like a monkey", as if Jekyll is evolving backwards.

A picture of an ape-like image of Charles Darwin and a real ape.

Before psychology
In the story, Stevenson explores the possibility of divisions within the mind. His idea foreshadowed later psychological investigations, as scientists began to probe the human mind.

Jekyll's drug
At the time this story was written, there was increasing anxiety about drugs. Jekyll begins with an experiment and ends up reliant on his potion – a frightening parallel of drug addiction.

19th-century scientific equipment

THE LITERARY VERSUS THE LEGENDARY
The legend of Jekyll and Hyde differs in a number of ways from Stevenson's original. We do not even say Jekyll's name the way his creator wanted us to: Stevenson pronounced it "Jeekyll", because "Hyde and Jeekyll" sounds like "hide and seek".

Hyde the Ripper
The Hyde of legend is more of a beast than the Hyde of Stevenson's story. This dates back to 1888, when a brilliant play of *Dr Jekyll and Mr Hyde* was playing in London at the same time as Jack the Ripper did his notorious murders there. The two stories became linked in the public mind.

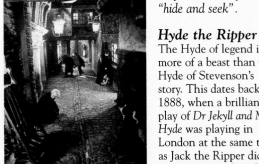

A recreation of one of the streets through which the Ripper prowled

Hyde on stage
A year after the book was published, the first stage version toured the USA to great applause. There have since been many successful stage productions, including a hit Broadway musical.

A poster for a stage play of Dr Jekyll and Mr Hyde.

The classic film

The most famous film version of *Dr Jekyll and Mr Hyde* is the 1932 film, directed by Rouben Mamoulian, starring Fredric March in the title roles. Fast-moving, with clever camera-work, it is a classic horror film.

Fredric March as Mr Hyde

Fredric March as Doctor Jekyll

Henry Jekyll and Edward Hyde were made for the big screen. The numerous film versions have usually introduced women and made the story more sensational. Films can never, however, portray Hyde as he is in the book, where his physical appearance is left to the imagination.

Spencer Tracy as Hyde (left) and Jekyll (right)

Famous stars

Spencer Tracy played the title roles in a 1941 film. His co-stars were Ingrid Bergman, as a barmaid, and Lana Turner as Jekyll's fiancée – the original book does not include either of those characters. A 1953 spoof, *Abbott and Costello meet Dr Jekyll and Mr Hyde,* starred the two American comics, and Boris Karloff, who was already famous for his portrayal of Frankenstein's monster.

A PARAMOUNT ARTCRAFT PICTURE

ADOLPH ZUKOR

John Barrymore "DR. JEKYLL AND MR. HYDE"

Silent film idol John Barrymore starred in a 1921 adaptation.

LIKE NOTHING YOU HAVE EVER SEEN! A COMPLETELY DIFFERENT VERSION OF THE CLASSIC STORY...A NEW DR. JEKYLL...A HANDSOME, EVIL MR. HYDE! **A SHOCK ENDING THAT YOU DARE NOT REVEAL!**

HOUSE of FRIGHT IN COLOR AND MEGASCOPE

A 1960 British film, The Two Faces of Doctor Jekyll, was released in the USA as House of Fright.

Twisting the plot

Variations on the story include *Son of Dr Jekyll* (1951), *Daughter of Dr Jekyll* (1957), and *The Nutty Professor* (1963) in which a drug turned a scientist into a pop star. The *Two Faces of Doctor Jekyll* (1960) made Hyde better-looking than Jekyll.

I, Monster (1971) stayed close to the original plot but changed all the names.

Alterations

Some films completely rewrite the story. In *Doctor Jekyll and Sister Hyde* (1971), Dr Jekyll turned into a woman. In *Mary Reilly,* (1996) Julia Roberts (right), played Jekyll's maid, a part invented for her. John Malkovich (left) played Jekyll and Hyde.

Acknowledgements

Picture Credits
The publisher would like to thank the following for their kind permission to reproduce the photographs.

t=top, b=bottom, a=above, c=centre, l=left, r=right.

Barnaby's Picture Library: 14cl; **Bridgeman Art Library, London:** Christie's, London 9tc, 11cr, 12bl; Christopher Wood Gallery, London 24bl; City of Edinburgh Museums and Art Galleries 60bl, 60/61bc; Courtesy of the Board of Trustees of the V&A 8cl (below); Department of the Environment, London 6/7c; Guildhall Library, Corporation of London 59tr; John Hay Whitney Collection, New York 61tr; Private Collection 14bl; Victorian Society, Linley Sambourne House, London 20bl; **Christie's Images, London:** 8tr, 10tl, 11tr, 18cl, 23tr, 28bl, 60tr (below), 62cl; Courtesy of **Coutts & Co., London:** 13tr; **Mary Evans Picture Library:** 2tc, 8tl, 9tr, 9cr, 14tl, 15tr, 18tl, 23cr, 31tr, 35tr, 37cr, 60tl, 60tl (below), 60c, 61cl, 61cr, 61bl, 61bc, 62tc, 62c, 62cr; **Hulton Getty:** 9cl, 20cl; **Ronald Grant Archive:** *Mary Reilly*, 1995 © Columbia Tristar 63br; **Robert Harding Picture Library:** Robert Francis 32tl;

Kobal Collection: *Doctor Jekyll and Mr Hyde*, 1941 © MGM 62tl, 63tl, 63tc, 63tr; *The Two Faces of Doctor Jekyll* 63c; *I Monster* 63bc; Courtesy of **Madame Tussaud's, London:** 62bl; **Mander & Mitchenson:** 62bc; **National Gallery of Scotland:** *Ordination of the Elders* John Henry Lorimar; Courtesy of the **Royal Mint:** 13tr; **Telegraph Colour Library:** 37br; By Courtesy of the Board of Trustees of the **Victoria and Albert Museum:** 42bl; **The Vintage Magazine Co.:** *Dr. Jekyll and Mr. Hyde*, 1932 © Turner Entertainment Co. 63cl, *Dr. Jekyll and Mr. Hyde*, 1921 © by Universal City Studios, Inc. Courtesy of Universal Studios Publishing Rights. All Rights Reserved. 63cr; **The Writers' Museum, Edinburgh:** 61tl.

Jacket: **Worthing Museum and Art Gallery:** front tl; **Mary Evans Picture Library:** back tc, back cl, inside back tc.

Photography: Andy Crawford at the DK Studio
Additional photography: Liz McAulay, Clive Streeter

Additional illustrations: Malcolm Chandler, Stephen Raw, Sallie Alane Reason

---

Dorling Kindersley would particularly like to thank the following people:

Angels & Bermans; Fergus Day, Elizabeth Bacon, and Emily Edlynn for research assistance; Natascha Biebow, Alastair Dougall, and Nick Turpin for editorial assistance; Arthur Middleton Antique Scientific Instruments; Sheilagh Noble for visualization.
Models: Martin Andrews, Céline Carez, Julie Ferris, Nigel Hill, Sacha Zdravkovic